To Arno, my sailing partner in fine and stormy weather. —MP

To Leo and Dina, our partners in laughter and mischief on the North Shore. —DG

Many thanks to Lee Radzak of Split Rock Lighthouse, the keeper's children who recorded their childhood recollections, Vicki and Steve Palmquist, Shannon Pennefeather, Pamela McClanahan, Dan Leary, and all the fine MNHS Press people, and to David Geister for bringing early-twentieth-century Split Rock to glorious life. —MP

I could not have created these paintings without my wonderful models, Aubrie, Allie, Matt, and my dear wife, Pat. Thanks to Lee Radzak for sharing his vast knowledge of Split Rock Lighthouse. Thanks also to Aaron Novodvorsky for his usual wisdom. —DG

THE PUBLICATION OF THIS BOOK WAS SUPPORTED IN PART THOUGH A GENEROUS GRANT FROM THE ELMER L. AND ELEANOR ANDERSEN PUBLICATIONS FUND.

The illustrations were created with oil paint on illustration board.

www.mnhspress.org

The Minnesota Historical Society Press is a member of the Association of American University Presses.

Manufactured in Canada

Book design by Brian Donahue / bedesign, inc.

10 9 8 7 6 5 4 3 2 1

∞ The paper used in this publication meets the minimum requirements of the American National Standard for Information Sciences—Permanence for Printed Library Materials, ANSI Z39.48-1984.

International Standard Book Number
ISBN: 978-1-68134-018-0 (cloth)

Library of Congress Cataloging-in-Publication Data available upon request.

STORM'S COMING!

Margi Preus

Illustrations by
David Geister

MINNESOTA
HISTORICAL
SOCIETY PRESS

"My!" Mama said as Sophie came into the kitchen. "This bread dough is rising fast!"

"Maybe there's a storm coming!" Sophie exclaimed.

"That's true." Mama eyed the puffy dough. "Bread always rises faster before a storm."

"I better warn Papa!" Sophie cried.

"All right," Mama said. "But first, tell Dan to bring in some wood for the cookstove."

Sophie found Dan in the garden picking cucumbers.
"Mama wants you to bring in wood for the cookstove.
Storm's coming!"

"How do you know?"

"Look at those busy bees," Sophie exclaimed. "*They* know it's going to storm."

Dan watched the bees flying into their hive. "That's true," he said. "You know what they say: *A bee was never caught in a shower.*"

"I have to warn Papa!" Sophie hopped up and down on one foot.

"First," Dan said, "you better tell Polly to take the sheets off the clothesline."

Sophie ran to the yard, where Polly was hanging laundry.
"Storm's coming!" Sophie said.
"Are you sure?" Polly asked.

Sophie picked a dandelion and held it up.

"Right!" Polly said. "Dandelion blossoms close up before a rain."

"So you better take the sheets off the line, and fast!" Sophie said. "I have to warn Papa!"

As Sophie raced off, Polly called after her, "Maybe you better tell Elizabeth to come home from blueberry picking!"

Wind billowed Sophie's skirt as she sprinted to the blueberry patch. Elizabeth sat in the middle, picking lots of plump and juicy berries.

"Storm's coming!" Sophie said.

"Really?" Elizabeth asked.

"That spider thinks so," Sophie said, pointing. "Look at that web. See how the frame lines are short and stout?"

"That's true," Elizabeth agreed. "She's making her web strong; wind and rain are coming."

"You better go home right away," Sophie said. "I have to warn Papa."

Elizabeth scampered off, calling over her shoulder, "Tell Tim and Ted to come in off the lake and pull up the boat."

Leaves twisted and fluttered in the cool breeze as
Sophie skittered down the steep stairway to the lake.
"Storm!" Sophie hollered to Tim and Ted.
"What?" Tim yelled back.

Sophie pointed at the gulls swooping near the water, and the boys started to row for shore.

"You know what they say," Ted said while Tim tied the boat. *"If birds fly low, then rain we shall know."*

"I have to warn Papa!" Sophie said.

"That's a good idea," the boys agreed.

Sophie hiked up the big hill under darkening skies. She rushed to the oil house, where she found Papa filling cans with gasoline.

"Papa! Papa!" she cried. "Storm's coming!"

"Is that so?" Papa asked, yanking on the door.

"Listen to what that catchy door has to say."

Papa put his ear to the door. *"Catchy door and sticky drawer,"* he said, *"coming rain will pour and pour."*

"We better make sure the foghorn is ready," Sophie said, "in case it gets foggy."

Sophie helped Papa lug the gasoline cans to the
fog signal building, where Papa poured the fuel into
the engine that made the foghorn blow.

"Now," Papa said, "you better run along home."

"Yes," Sophie agreed, "but Papa, shouldn't we
make sure the light is all set, in case it gets very dark
during the storm?"

Papa sighed and said, "All right, then."

Sophie followed him up the thirty-two stairs of the lighthouse. She checked the windows as she climbed, making sure each one was shut tight. Glancing out, she saw black clouds moving across the sky. The lake below was a shifting pattern of green and black and purple.

At the top, Sophie helped wind the clock that kept the lens turning on time.

Then Papa said, "Now you better run home."

"But Papa," Sophie said, "shouldn't we polish the lens to make sure the light is bright for the stormy night ahead?"

"*I'll* polish the lens." Papa took out his special cloth. "It has to be done just so. *You* better run along home!"

"Oh, no, Papa! I can't. I have to stay here with you."

"Why?" Papa asked.

"Because . . ." Sophie began.

Just then, a big jagged flash lit the sky, thunder
boomed, and rain lashed against the windows.
Sophie smiled up at Papa. "It's storming!"

Author's Note

In the days before radio, TV, and smartphones, the children who lived at Split Rock Lighthouse got their weather forecast from the world of nature right outside their door. One of those children, Beulah Covell-Myers, said the keepers "were very cognizant of the weather. They would have to watch for signs and weather changes. Those things were passed on to us kids."

Storms were easy to spot when they swept across the lake from the northeast. But sometimes, as in this story, storms crept over the hills from *behind* the lighthouse. Those storms, known by local fishermen as "dirty nor'westers" would just suddenly appear, making them especially dangerous, particularly for anyone who had ventured out onto the water. So it was helpful to be able to read other weather signs, and it's likely the children of Split Rock were familiar with the proverbs in this story. But are these proverbs based on fact or fiction?

Bread makers know that when the barometric pressure is low (as it typically is before a storm) the dough doesn't have as much air to "push" against, so it rises faster.

Bees seek shelter before it rains, probably because water droplets add weight and cause their wings to stick together, making it harder to fly.

Dandelions and tulips close up before a rain, protecting their nectar and pollen from getting washed away.

Spiders have been observed strengthening their webs, or even taking them down before storms.

Birds are very sensitive to barometric pressure. Some are known to fly lower in the sky before rain.

There is still a lot we don't know about *how* it is that some plants and creatures seem to know the weather is about to change, we only know they *do*!

There are many more weather forecasting proverbs. Can you think of some?